Gemma & Gus

Olivier Dunrea

HOUGHTON MIFFLIN HARCOURT
Boston   New York

To access the read-along audio file, visit
WWW.HMHBOOKS.COM/FREEDOWNLOADS
ACCESS CODE: EXPLORE

AGES	GRADES	GUIDED READING LEVEL	READING RECOVERY LEVEL	LEXILE® LEVEL
4-6	1	E	7-8	230L

The text was set in Shannon. The illustrations are pen-and-ink and gouache on 140-pound d'Arches coldpress watercolor paper.

The Library of Congress Cataloging-in-Publication Data is on file.

ISBN: 978-0-544-93722-2 paperback
ISBN: 978-0-544-93680-5 paper-over-board

Manufactured in China
SCP 10 9 8 7 6 5 4 3 2 1
4500635249

To Dani, the bravest explorer I know

This is Gemma.

This is Gus.

Gemma is a small yellow gosling.
She is the big sister.

Gus is a smaller yellow gosling.
He is the little brother.

Gemma likes to explore
new places.

Gus follows.

Gemma hunts for frogs
in the cattails.

Gus hunts too.

Gemma looks for bunnies
hiding in the oak tree.

Gus looks too.

Gemma hops onto the
flowerpot.

Gus hops up too.

Gemma climbs on top
of Molly.

Gus climbs up too.

"Don't keep following me!"
Gemma honks.

Gus peeks underneath
the hen.

Gemma peeks too.

Gus looks down from
the flowerpot.

Gemma looks down too.

Gus jumps into the pond.

Gemma jumps too.

Gus splashes in the pond.

Gemma splashes too.

Gus scoots to a large rock.

"WHAT ARE YOU DOING?"
Gemma honks.
"EXPLORING!" honks Gus.

This is Gemma.

This is Gus.

Gemma and Gus are two small goslings who like to explore—together.